H. E. Kramer

## Entertainments for Church Socials

women's social and charitable organizations, juvenile and young people's

societies, and private parties

H. E. Kramer

**Entertainments for Church Socials**
*women's social and charitable organizations, juvenile and young people's societies, and private parties*

ISBN/EAN: 9783337370671

Printed in Europe, USA, Canada, Australia, Japan

Cover: Foto ©Andreas Hilbeck / pixelio.de

More available books at **www.hansebooks.com**

# ENTERTAINMENTS

—FOR—

## CHURCH SOCIALS,

## Women's Social and Charitable Organizations,

JUVENILE & YOUNG PEOPLE'S SOCIETIES.

—AND—

## PRIVATE PARTIES,

AKRON, O.:

MRS. H. E. KRAMER.

1892.

# Entertainments.

- — -

## Festival of Roses.

"Oh! What is so sweet as a rose in June!"

The Festival of Roses is a beautiful entertainment for the month of June, and has delighted all who have seen it. It is attended with but little expense, and must be given when roses are just in their prime. Let a large committee be appointed to solicit roses— the cut flowers, (who that has them will not share them for a benevolent enterprise?) also trailing vines of all kinds, and ferns.

From these, select the choicest and put aside to be made into hand and button-hole bouquets and sold.

If possible, give the entertainment in one large, rather than in several small rooms, as less material will be required for decorating, and the general effect will be more pleasing.

For decorations use festoons of cheese cloth of the colors of roses— pink, red, white, yellow, cream and rose.

After this is arranged, pin, with common dressing pins, roses of all colors, also vines and fern leaves at intervals on the drapery.

The cheese cloth can be sold after the entertainment, or laid aside to be used on another occasion.

If the room is not carpeted, a home-like effect is obtained by placing rugs here and there on the floor, and having rockers, easels, etc., arranged as in a parlor.

In each of the four corners of the room arrange a booth. and drape the same with old lace curtains, upon which also pin roses, vines and ferns. In one of these, strawberries and ice cream will be served—in another, lemonade—in the third have hand and button-hole bouquets. while the fourth will serve as a candy booth. Use plenty of roses in decorating. Bouquets and baskets of roses should be *everywhere*.

Each lady participating, either in the program. in serving refreshments, or in any other way must assume the name of a rose, as "Baltimore Belle," or "Princess Marechal Neil," by which name she will be known during the evening, and must wear a dress the color of that rose, or white, with corsage bouquet of roses the name of which she assumes.

If gentlemen assist. each of them also assumes the name of a rose, as. "Prince Camille de Rohen" and wear buttonhole bouquet of same. The following list of names, with corresponding colors. will be found helpful in choosing names:

| | |
|---|---|
| Princess Adelaide, | pink. |
| Catherine Mermet, | pink. |
| Baltimore Belle, | white. |
| Prairie Queen, | rose. |
| Perfection Des Blanches, | white. |
| Caroline De Sansal, | light pink. |
| Annie De Diesbach. | carmine. |
| Baroness Rothschild, | light pink. |
| Her Majesty, | pink. |
| Bella, | white. |
| Blanche Moreau, | white. |
| Coquette De Lyn, | yellow. |
| Duchess of Edinburg. | red. |
| Duchess De Brabant, | rose. |
| Etoile De Lyon, | yellow. |
| Marie Guillot, | white. |
| Marechal Neil, | yellow. |

| | |
|---|---|
| American Beauty, | deep rose. |
| George the Fourth, | crimson, |
| General Washington, | crimson, |
| General Jacqueminot, | dark crimson. |
| Baron De Bonstetter, | dark red. |
| Victor Verdier, | bright rose. |
| Henry Martin, | pink. |
| Douglas, | red. |
| Charles Rovolli, | rose. |

Other names can be added at the suggestion of a florist.

A neatly printed program is provided, having two perforations at the upper left hand corner, through which a tiny moss rosebud is placed. This also makes a pretty souvenir for each guest.

The programs should be distributed by two little girls, wearing white dresses elaborately trimmed with rosebuds and half blown roses. They may also assist in disposing of button-hole bouquets.

Following is the program:

| | |
|---|---|
| Short Talk | "War of Roses" |
| Vocal Solo | "Last Rose of Summer" |
| Recitation | "Brier Rose" |
| Chorus | "Rose of Sharon" |

Other numbers may be added if a lengthy program is desired. This entertainment was given in one of the large city churches, to the delight of hundreds who attended, and netted a handsome sum

All decorations, except pinning on the roses, can be arranged at pleasure, while that should be deferred until within a few hours of the program. The roses and vines will not wither sufficiently to be noticeable in the evening, when, with bright lights, the effect is charming.

An admission of twenty-five or thirty cents is charged.

including ice-cream and strawberries, other refreshments
being extra, or charge ten cents admission, with an extra
charge for all refreshments.

### Observation Party.

At an Observation Party each guest is given five cards,
with representations of the five senses printed upon them.
At a given signal, instruments of various kinds are played
upon in an adjoining room and at the end of a half minute
each guest is to write the name of as many of them as he
recognized, on his card on which is printed the *ear*.

The one having the largest number is awarded a prize.

In the contest for the sense of seeing, the guests are
taken into a room where numerous objects were placed upon
a table—they glanced at it for half a minute, retired, and
each wrote the names of the articles seen, upon the card
representing the *eye*.

They are then given to taste of a mixture of various
ingredients, and each makes note of the number of articles
tasted, and writes the result upon the card representing the
*tongue*. The guests are then blindfolded and are given
various articles to distinguish by the sense of touch, writing
the results as before.

Lastly, bottles containing liquids, easily distinguished,
were placed before the guests, each one to determine by the
sense of smell, what was contained in the bottles, writing
the results on the card representing the *nose*.

In each case prizes are given to the successful contest-
ants.

## Library Social.

A Library Social was recently given with great success, by the members of a young ladies' society. in the spacious, double parlors of one of the members. The young ladies in charge were "mum" in regard to the nature of the entertainment—simply inviting their gentlemen friends to a Library Social at a certain time and place.

They suggested also that the gentlemen meet at an appointed place. and attend the social *en masse*.

Upon their arrival they are met by the president of the society, or any person appointed. who welcomes them, stating also that she has in her library a choice collection of valuable books which she is going to give them the privilege of examining.

She then introduces the Librarian and an assistant, who furnish the gentlemen with dainty cards containing a list of the books. or catalogue.

No one is allowed to keep a book more than five minutes. In case they do. they will be liable to a fine of a cent a minute. The librarian will keep an account of time. The library is separated from the guest room by sliding doors, or portieres.

Applications for books are now made to the librarian from the following catalogue:

No. 1. Under the Lilacs.
" 2. Old Fashioned Girl.
" 3. Hidden Hand.
" 4. A Fair Barbarian.
" 5. Samantha at Saratoga.
" 6. Rose in Bloom.
" 7. Little Women.
" 8. Under Two Flags.
" 9. Songs in Many Keys.

No. 10.　Pink and White Tyranny.
"　11.　Woman in White.
"　12.　Scarlet Letter.
"　13.　Ivanhoe.
"　14.　Madcap Violet.
"　15.　Views Afoot.
"　16.　Little Red Riding Hood.
"　17.　Romola.
"　18.　Aunt Jo's Scrap Bag.
"　19.　Pioneer.
"　20.　The Moonstone.
"　21.　The Last of the Tribunes.
"　22.　Jane Eyre.
"　23.　The Newcombs.
"　24.　History of Greece.
"　25.　The Snow Image.

The list may be enlarged at pleasure.　As has probably been surmised, each young lady impersonates one of the books, and, as applications are made for them, the librarian disappears behind the portieres and produces them, bringing them forward to the person calling for them.

For instance, No. 11 is called for, which is represented by a pretty young lady dressed in white. 'No. 3, "Hidden Hand," appears with one hand hidden in a muff, or in the folds of her gown.　No. 9, "Songs in Many Keys," appears with a number of pieces of music, each in a different key. No. 21 produces a copy of the New York Tribune, last edition.　No. 12 wears a letter of scarlet pasteboard instead of a brooch.　No. 25 wears a dress of white covered with bits of cotton batting.　At the expiration of the alloted time, each book is returned to the library and put at the disposal of others.

In this way, the parlors are filled with a gay company of conversationalists, during the entire evening, the constant drawing and changing of books making a delightful evening for all. Of course, as each book is produced from the library, all guess as to the title, while the gentleman calling for the book, has "her" for a partner for five minutes.

Light refreshments are served during the evening.

-------⋆----  -

### Longfellow Evening.

Song—"The Bridge."
Short talk—"Life of Longfellow."
Song—"The Village Blacksmith."
Story from the works of Longfellow.
Reading—"Song of Hiawatha."
Song—"The Day is Done."

For the "story," select a person to recite or read an original story, using, in a connected way, the titles of his different poems. Like this— At the close of "A Rainy Day" in "Autumn," I sat by "The Open Window" etc., etc. Or, select say six persons each to write such a "story," giving a copy of Longfellow's Poems to the one who in his story uses the largest number of titles of poems. During the reading of the "Song of Hiawatha," have a number of tableaux, which will add greatly to the interest.

The tableaux may be as follows:

"The Wigwam of Nokomis."
"Youthful Hiawatha."
"Hiawatha leaving to wed Laughing Water."
"Arrow-maker and Minnehaha."
"Welcoming Hiawatha."
"Beautiful Minnehaha."
"Nokomis and Minnehaha waiting for Hiawatha."
"Famine and Fever."
"Dying Minnehaha."

"Return of Hiawatha."
"Mourning Hiawatha."

If refreshments are desired, serve assorted nuts, candies and macaroons, in small baskets, at fifteen cents each.

An admission is charged at the door.

— — — —:— — — —

## B., L. and O. Festival.

One of the prettiest of "color affairs" is a banana, lemon, and orange festival. Two apartments only are necessary for giving this entertainment.

One large supper room where the program can also be given, and a smaller, yet commodious room for the sale of articles.

For the supper room arrange as many long tables as will accommodate the number of guests expected.

Use white tablecloths and napkins and around the edge of both baste a "frill" of crimped lemon or orange colored tissue paper.

Put each napkin in a glass, at each plate. The table cloth is caught up here and there around the edges and fastened with little bows of ribbon.

Make numerous mats and doylies of the colored papers for each table, using no colored glass or china on the tables, unless it be of one of the colors of the evening.

Festoons of the colored paper should reach from the chandelier to each table. In the center of each table arrange a dish of oranges, lemons and bananas cut in fanciful shapes, while at either end there should be a bowl of flowers. The ladies in charge of the tables wear lemon or orange colored gowns with white aprons, caps and neckerchiefs. Orange colored cheese cloth or print will do nicely for the dresses.

Serve a cold supper consisting of meats, salads, pickles, jellies and cheese, and the following:

| | |
|---|---|
| Orange Cake | Lemon Custard |
| Lemon Cake | Orange Pudding |
| Banana Cake | Orange Float |
| Lemon Wafers | Lemon Jelly |

Sliced Oranges and Cocoanut
Sliced Bananas with Cream
Banana, Orange and Lemon Ice-cream
Orange and Lemon Ices. Lemonade
Tea and Coffee

Have sliced lemon at each plate for those who wish to use it in their tea. Arrange the "salesroom" as prettily as possible, using lace curtains and lemon and orange colored draperies. In the center arrange a " B., L. and O. Stand," by suspending a huge umbrella, covered inside and out, with the colored tissue paper, with festoons of same around the edges. Then hang lemons, oranges and bananas, by yellow cord or ribbon, all around.

Under the umbrella have a table for the sale of same, either singly, or by the dozen, at prices charged by grocers.

Solicit donations of colored tissue papers articles, consisting of mats, flowers and lamplighters, also crotched mats, throws, or any fancy article in which the colors of the evening predominate.

Arrange one corner of the room for serving lemonade and cake, using a lemonade set consisting of large glass bowl, with silver ladle, and several dozen cups.

Ice cream and ices are served in another part of the room.

Many will want light refreshments who cannot come to supper.

The ladies in charge will wear costumes similar to those in the supper room.

Any good musical or literary program may be given in the evening.

Another feature of this entertainment is a "B., L. and O. Tree."

Where a lemon or orange tree cannot be had, an oleander or evergreen will do. Make fifty or one hundred oranges, lemons, and bananas, out of card board covered with silesia. Put in each one a useful article worth a quarter, sew up, and hang on the tree.

After the program, announce that this "fruit" is for sale at twenty-five cents a piece. You will be surprised to find how quickly the tree will be stripped of its fruit.

If printed invitations are issued let them be upon lemon and orange colored cards, or white, with a fanciful design of the fruit, in water colors, done by the artist members of the society.

Charge twenty-five cents for supper and program.

Those not coming to supper can be served to what they wish after the program.

--- ❖ --- ---

### Bean Bag Party.

This entertainment is perhaps best given on a lawn, though a large hall will answer nicely.

The first thing to provide is several sets of the game—"Bean Bags."

Each set consists of the board, eight small bean bags, and one large one. To make the board, take a smooth, pine board, eighteen inches wide and twenty-seven long, and plane off the edges nicely. Ten inches from the top of the board, and in the middle, cut out a space four and a half by six and a half inches.

Nine inches from the top and on the under side of the board, put on with hinges, another board ten inches by eight inches high. This will slant the board at a proper angle so the bags can be thrown through the hole. When this is done, either paint the board red, and stripe it with black, or oil it, and stripe it with bright colors.

For the bags, take cretonne or bright striped ticking and make eight bags three by four inches, and one, "Jumbo," four by six inches. Then fill all, scantily, with beans and sew up the ends.

Both board and bags are cheaply and easily made, and the game affords no end of amusement.

To play the game, place the board fifteen feet in front of the players. Let the first player take the nine bags and try to throw each one through the hole in the board.

The game is *one hundred*.

Each small bag, if it goes through the hole, counts *ten*. If it remains on the board it counts *five*. If it falls off, or does not hit the board at all, it *takes off five*.

"Jumbo," if it goes through the hole counts *twenty*. If it remains on the board it counts *ten*. If it falls off, or fails to hit the board, it *takes off ten*.

Any number can play, each player in turn, taking the nine bags, and throwing all of them, before giving place to the next.

Each person may count for himself, or let a person be selected to count for all. A different person may be chosen to have charge of each set during the evening, explaining the game to the players, and settling any points of difference that may arise.

The game is interesting for old and young, and with refreshments, will furnish a pleasant evening's entertainment.

If given in the winter, serve a New England supper, charging twenty-five cents for supper, and privilege of playing game.

If in summer, light, cooling refreshments can be served from attractive little booths on the lawn. In this case, charge an admission of ten cents, refreshments being extra.

———————:———————

### Bachelors' Banquet.

In the Bachelors' Banquet is found a pleasing variation from the ordinary social.

The ladies especially will appreciate the change, inasmuch as *they* will be the guests, while their husbands, brothers, lovers and friends will entertain them during the evening and serve them to all the delicacies that the elaborate bill of fare provides.

The gentlemen must have exclusive charge of the whole affair, preparing and serving the repast and washing the dishes.

A musical and literary program is given, one feature of which is a paper—"The Bachelor's Budget," whose editorial staff must be chosen by the chairman of the general committee of arrangements.

The "Budget" is devoted to the best interests of bachelors, giving helpful hints on keeping "bachelors' hall," choice recipes, etc. Its columns may also contain items of general and personal interest.

Special committees are appointed as follows: General Committee of Arrangements, Invitation Committee, Program

Committee, Refreshment Committee, Reception Committee and Waiters. The latter wear white caps and aprons.

Cheaply printed invitations on sheets of manilla paper of the size of note are issued, and also contain the program and menu.

The program may be a burlesque, or at least should be droll, and out of the ordinary. Following is the

### MENU.

#### FISH.

| | |
|---|---|
| White Fish. | [In the Market.] |
| Gold Fish. | [In the Aquarium.] |
| Fresh Fish. | [In the Lake.] |
| Minnows. | [In the Brook.] |

#### GAME.

| | |
|---|---|
| Rabbits. | [In the Hedge. |
| Quail. | [In the Brush.] |
| Copenhagen. | Drop the Handkerchief. |
| Blind Man's Buff. | Hide and Seek. |

#### COLD DISHES.

Broken Ice.  Sliced Lemons with Vinegar.  Stewed Icicles.
Tongue.  Cold Ice.
Mother-in-Law, with Son-in-Law Sass.

#### DRINKS.

No Tea.  No Soda Water.  No Lemonade.  Hard Water.
Soft Water.  Hydrant Water.  Ice Water.
Chocolate and Coffee.

#### WAFFLES.

| | |
|---|---|
| Waffles Hot. | Waffles Cold. |
| Waffles Plain. | Waffles Buttered. |
| Waffles, with Syrup. | Doughnuts. |

### SCALE OF PRICES.
#### TERMS CASH.

| | | |
|---|---|---|
| Waffles, with Syrup | - - - - - - | 5 cents |
| Doughnuts | - - - - - - - | 2 for 5 cents |
| Coffee | - 5 cents  Chocolate - - | 5 cents |

Eat all you want and pay for what you eat.

As will be seen, all that is really served is waffles, doughnuts, coffee and chocolate.

The following notes should also be printed on the invitations:

1.  Ladies are warned to keep out of the culinary department.

2.  Waffles and doughnuts will be manufactured by the Refreshment Committee, and are warranted to be indigestible.

3.  No oleomargarine will be used, but the good, honest article instead, of sufficient strength and color for the occasion.

4.  Reliable and well known remedies for dyspepsia and indigestion will be on sale, at reduced rates, during the evening.

————·❖·

### Experience Social.

Where societies desire to swell their treasuries by direct giving instead of by means of entertainments, and where a uniform plan is desired the following methods have been recently tried with great success. One by a children's society, the other by a society of ladies, each numbering over one hundred members.

The children were each given a bright new penny, with instructions to invest and increase it as a business man does his capital.

Each was to devise his own way, and at the end of a given time, two or three months, to return it, with the increase—whether ten, fifty, or one hundred fold, and upon presenting it, to relate his or her experience in increasing it. Perhaps no two will have adopted the same method.

One boy bought a penny's worth of popcorn, which he popped and sold for five cents. With this he bought more, popped it, and sold it, realizing one dollar and ten cents.

An industrious girl borrowed four cents from her

mother, and bought half a yard of ticking which she made
into holders, selling them at five and ten cents each. With
the proceeds she bought more, and continued selling till she
cleared two dollars.

Another girl bought a penny's worth of bright flannel
from her mother, and made a pretty penwiper which she
sold for ten cents. She then bought tissue paper of pretty
colors and made fancy lamp lighters, increasing her penny
to fifty cents.

A boy earned four cents to put with his penny, and
bought a box of blacking, and blacked his father's shoes
for a month, realizing a dollar and a half.

In the ladies' society, each one pledged herself to earn
a dollar in a given time, and in presenting it, to give her
experience in raising it. Many wrote their experiences in
verse, which was doubly interesting. Here is a sample
verse:

> " I earned my dollar—baked the bread,
> , Dusted rooms and made the bed;
> Washed the dishes, blacked the stove,
> Doing work that least I love." etc.

Here's another:

> " Now, my dear friends, if you would know
> How I my dollar sought to grow —
> By planting "taters" on our lot,
> And fighting bugs at every spot."

Another:

> " Thus all my bread in cash was paid,
> And here I bring the measure
> Of two bright dimes, paid just five times,
> Which makes the dollar treasure."

Others earned the dollar by "writing poetry," burning
rubbish off the back yard, selling cookies, blacking their
husband's shoes, doctoring a son's sick horse, trimming

hats, selling kindling wood, making jelly, baking pies, mending chairs, washing the buggy, sprinkling the lawn, and doing fancy sewing, while one denied herself twenty street car rides.

--------- ⁂ ---------

### Dolls' Reception.

A score or more of bright girls of twelve years of age, or under, under the supervision of their mothers, can make the Dolls' Reception a novel and delightful entertainment. First, secure the loan for one evening of ''all the dolls in town,'' of all ages, shapes and sizes, complexions and climes. You want big and little dolls, old and new dolls, black and white dolls, lady dolls, babies, sailor boys and sailor girls, rag dolls, rubber dolls, bisque and china dolls, wax dolls and paper dolls, aged dolls, broken dolls, crying dolls and laughing dolls. On little slips of paper write the name of each person to whom the dolls belong, and pin it on the doll's clothing out of sight.

If this is done there will be no mistakes, and each doll can be carefully returned to its owner, after the reception is over.

Numerous articles of doll furniture will also be needed. In the room where the reception is held, arrange a number of tables of various sizes on which to exhibit the dolls.

Let each table represent the room of a doll's house. These are tastefully furnished with doll furniture, and are ''occupied'' by dolls, suitably dressed, that have been loaned. There can be a drawing room, bed room, dining room, kitchen, nursery and playroom. Arrange also a hospital, where all dolls bereft of an arm, a leg, a nose, or an eye, or in any way injured, will be cared for by trained doll nurses, in white caps and aprons. Aged rag dolls may also be sheltered in the hospital.

With the aid of doll hammocks, swings, carriages, and chairs, a pretty garden scene can be arranged.

Of the numerous articles of doll furniture now made, nearly every child possesses one or more pieces, so that all that is required for each room can easily be gotten.

The girls giving the entertainment will receive the guests as they arrive, and conduct them to the various apartments, and afterwards show them to seats.

A program of songs and recitations is then given by the girls, every number of which must pertain to dolls. Material for this can be procured from any of the leading children's magazines and books. After the program, arrange for them to serve a light, dainty lunch.

Charge 15 cents for reception and program, or 25 cents, including lunch.

———◦———

### Stand Up Supper.

An inexpensive and novel way of serving refreshments at a private party, is by having a Stand Up Supper.

In the supper room arrange two long tables, both handsomely furnished, with fine linen, china and glass.

Instead of laying a plate for each guest, set the plates in half dozens here and there on the tables, also have a liberal supply of forks, spoons and glasses. Fruit and flowers upon the tables will add much to the effect.

For convenience, a cold supper is almost a necessity. Rolls, buns, sandwiches, salads, cold ham and tongue, pickles, jellies, custards, crackers and cheese, lemonade, ices, milk, cake and ice cream.

These are all placed upon the tables. tastefully arranged, when supper is announced.

Upon invitation. the guests. in an entirely informal way. proceed to the supper room. where each one helps himself to a plate. fork. and spoon. and to what he wishes. from the tables.    Or. the gentlemen may serve the ladies. and vice versa. the ladies may serve each other. or the young serve the older ones.

The supper is eaten standing by the tables. walking about the room. or in groups of half dozens.

Chairs are provided for those unable to stand. or several lunch tables can be added.

The expense of a corps of waiters is thus dispensed with. and. if the hostess has the faculty of making her guests feel at home. the supper is an assured success.

The supper room should be brilliantly lighted. and made attractive in every way.   After supper the guests return to the parlors. where they resume whatever entertainment has been provided.   The evening may be spent in games and conversation.

The affair is entirely informal. and while it affords a delightful evening. it relieves a hostess of much of the work attendant upon giving parties.

### Patriotic Festival.

A Patriotic Festival continues through an entire day. Serve dinner and supper and furnish evening entertainment.

As a means of thoroughly advertising it. and at the same time adding materially to the proceeds. have printed several thousand tissue paper flags. the size to be governed by the number of advertisements you expect to solicit.   The flags are white, with the stripes outlined with red, and the stars, and square space for same, outlined with blue. Each stripe is divided into little squares, for each of which you solicit an advertisement from business firms, charging, perhaps, two dollars each for them.

Each star must also contain an "ad"—the space here being more valuable. In the space for the stars must also be left room to announce the Festival, when and where held, entertainment furnished and prices. These "flags" are folded into pretty shapes, and are liberally distributed before and during the festival.

Dinner and supper tickets, also tickets for evening entertainment, represent tiny flags, and should be placed on sale several weeks before hand. This will also serve as a means of advertising.

The programs for the evening are printed on tiny flags, which each guest will keep as a souvenir.

Have an elaborate display of the national colors, in the hall where the Festival is held.

Tiny flags, arranged in fancy designs, are pretty upon the tables. If given in the summer, the table decorations are pretty of red, white, and blue flowers.

The ladies in charge may wear costumes of red, white and blue, or dark dresses, with "flag" caps and aprons.

Or, the costume may consist of skirt of turkey red, white bodice, and blue girdle, with white caps.

The following program is suitable:

Grand March...... . ................ .. ......Fifty little girls
Chorus, "Columbia"... . ...... ...... ........... " " "
　　　　　　　　　　　Tableau "Columbia."
Vocal Solo.......... . ................ ..."Star Spangled Banner"
Recitation...................... ............."Barbara Frietchie"
　　　　　Tableau—"Tenting on the Old Camp Ground."

Solo and Chorus .... ......" Tramp. Tramp. Tramp"
Fancy Flag Drill.... ...... .... ............. Fifty little girls
Quartette ..... ..... ................" Marching Through Georgia"
Tableau · " Poor Old Slave."
War Incidents.................. ........ ....... .Menfbers G. A. R.
Chorus............... .......................... " Yankee Doodle"
Tableau—" The Goodbye.
Solo and Chorus ...... ... " When Johnny Comes Marching"
Duet and Chorus ..... ......................." Brave Boys are They"
Tableau—" The Return"
Chorus........... ........................" Glory. Glory. Hallelujah"
Tableau—" Peace"

The fifty little girls are dressed in white. wearing shoulder sashes of red. white. and blue. each carrying a flag, which they wave. at the proper time. while singing.

For the fancy drill. they must have careful drill by an army officer. and must also be very familiar with the choruses.

The girls can greatly aid by selling tickets and passing programs. or they may act as ushers.

--------·--------

### Crayon Social.

A new and very amusing social is the one herein described.

Provide as many cards as guests are expected.

Of these. all are blanks except twenty. Of the latter. each one is numbered from one to twenty.

The twenty numbered cards are then indiscriminately mixed with the others. numbers down. so that no one can see which are numbered and which are blank. Provide twenty more cards of good size and of a different tint from the others.

On one side of these cards have "Crayon Social" prettily written or printed in gilt.

On the opposite side, in upper right-hand corner, write the numbers 1, 2, 3, etc., up to twenty, as on the other twenty cards, while down the left-hand side are *all* the numbers from 1 to 20, with sufficient space left to write the name of an animal opposite each number.

These cards should be made as pretty as possible.

A "teacher," previously appointed, now invites each guest in turn to draw a card from the first lot. The twenty persons who draw the numbered cards now constitute the "pupils," while those who have drawn blanks are the audience.

A good sized blackboard must be provided and colored crayons may be used.

The teacher now arranges his pupils before him in line, according to number, and gives to each, one of the fancy numbered cards.

He now calls for "No. 1" to come forward to the board where he stands, and tells him to draw an animal.

Just as No. 1 is ready to begin, the teacher tells him (in a whisper) *what* animal he is to draw, as the *dog, cat* or *horse.* When the picture is finished, No. 1 is again seated, while each of the remaining nineteen pupils write the name of the animal they *think* No. 1 has meant to represent on the board, opposite No. 1 on their card.

No. 2 is next called and told by his teacher what animal to draw, while each pupil writes the result as before.

When each of the twenty pupils has drawn an animal the teacher announces what animals he asked to have drawn and a prize is offered to the pupil who has guessed the largest number correctly.

The guessing is not always an easy matter, as not all

are artists. and no one knows till he is called forward what animal he is to draw.

Consequently the animals are sometimes sadly lacking the "features" which would make them recognizable.

## Feast of Days.

Similar to. yet differing from. a fair. is the Feast of Days.

Arrange as many booths as there are days in the week.

Above each. hang a printed card bearing the name of the day represented within. also a suitable motto.

Beginning with the *Sunday booth*—the motto "We Rest in Peace" hangs overhead. This booth is made as attractive and homelike as possible. while all articles on sale are suggestive of rest.

Chair cushions. fancy pillows. comfortables. rockers. hammocks. slumber robes. silk quilts. etc.. are on sale.

"Monday—Real Estate Transferred" is the significant motto which greets the visitor's eye as he approaches this booth The costumes of the attendants suggest that they are ready for the work of "blue Monday" while many useful "Monday articles" are on sale—tubs. washboards. boilers. clothes lines and clothes pins. wringers and soap.

"Tuesday—We Smooth All Wrinkles" announces the motto over the next booth. while within are found ironing boards. irons. stands. holders and clothes hampers.

"Wednesday—A Stitch in Time Saves Nine Mend Your Ways." Here are found darning cotton and needles. worsted yarns. thimbles. etc.

"Thursday Forget Not to Entertain Strangers." This booth represents a handsome reception room. with the hostesses waiting to welcome the guests. Various pieces of fancy work, bric-a-brac, rugs, pictures, tea sets, lunch tables and spreads in abundance are offered for sale.

"Friday A New Broom Sweeps Clean" is the time-worn saying over the next booth. Here the attendants are arrayed for sweeping and dusting, while they offer for sale brooms, whisk brooms, feather dusters, dust cloths, sweeping caps, aprons, dust pans and sweepers.

"Saturday The Way to a Man's Heart is Through His Stomach." Here a tempting lunch is served, and cake, candy, sandwiches, coffee, doughnuts and cookies, etc., are on sale.

This entertainment can be made as elaborate or as simple as desired, according to the numbers participating and of those from whom to solicit articles.

If given on a smaller scale, a private home would be a desirable place in which to hold it.

---  ❖

### Rainbow and Soap-Bubble Party.

Provide seven (or fourteen if necessary) lunch or sewing tables, each of which will seat six or eight persons. Use white lunch cloths, while the decoration of each table is one of the primary colors of the rainbow violet, indigo, blue, green, yellow, orange and red.

The ladies in charge of each table will wear shoulder sashes and caps of the color of their table decoration.

Provide several bowls of soap suds, to which a little glycerine has been added, for each table; also a fancy hand-decorated pipe for each guest.

After the social, the pipes may be sold at ten or fifteen cents each, or may be given as favors to each guest.

The early part of the evening may be spent in blowing bubbles. after which the bowls are removed and lunch is served from the same tables.

For the lunch, the following would be quickly served and prepared. and palatable:

Chocolate and Cake.              Wafers and Cheese. with Tea.
Coffee and Doughnuts.           Gingerbread and Milk.
                Lady Fingers and Lemonade.

A program is given by the young ladies in charge of the tables.

Charge a small admission for program and blowing bubbles. each guest choosing the refreshments he wishes and paying accordingly.

On the invitation cards should be printed in one corner. a rainbow. in another. a bowl of soap suds and pipe.

------------:-----------

### Dickens Party.

To be interesting. it is necessary that a large number of characters be represented in costume. even though but few take part in the program.   It is simply a "character party."   Each guests tries to recognize by the costume the character assumed by the others.

Any illustrated edition of Dickens will give the necessary ideas as to costume.

The following list of characters is suggested. having been used at a large and successful Dickens Party recently held.

Florence Dombey.          Jennie Wren,
Mrs. Jeleby.              Mrs. Jarley.
Mr. Squeers,              Dick Swiveller,
Mrs. Squeers.            Mr. Micawber.
Fannie Squeers,          Esther Summerson.

| | |
|---|---|
| Marchioness. | Laavy, the Irrepressible. |
| Mrs. Micawber. | Oliver Twist. |
| Grandfather. | Agnes. |
| Mrs. Pardiggle. | Toots. |
| Peggotty. | Dora. |
| Sam Weller. | Guppy. |
| Dot, | Mr. Dick. |
| Little Nell. | David Copperfield, |
| Pickwick. | Mr. Barkis. |
| Nicholas Nickleby. | Lady Deadlock. |
| Mrs. Wilfer. | Norleena Kenwigs. |

Have a program consisting of several musical selections. in addition to which, give the following:

Talk—" Dickens and His Works."
Dialogue—" Dick Swiveller and Marchioness."
Tableau —" Barkis is Willin'."
Dialogue—" Guppy's Avowal."
Tableau—" Death of Little Nell."
Dialogue— " Toots Presents Diogenes."
Wax Works— Mrs. Jarley.

Sandwiches and coffee. or chocolate and cake may be served after the program.

An admission of twenty-five cents is charged. including lunch.

———— —❖— ——

### A. B. C Social.

Five booths are necessary at an A. B. C Social. One for Aprons. one for Bags, one for Caps, one for candy and fruit, and one for light refreshments.

An Apron Booth must be well stocked with aprons of *all kinds.* plain and fancy.

Gingham and rubber aprons, sewing aprons 'with pockets, black silk aprons. with a conventional design outlined in colors across the bottom. hemstitched linen and drawn work aprons, mull and lace aprons, and children's aprons of all kinds.

For suggestions for the Bag Booth see Bag Sale described elsewhere.

In the Cap Booth have on sale sweeping caps of cambric, silk or silesia of all colors, pretty morning caps of various kinds, nurses' caps, black lace caps, babies' knitted and crotched caps, and boys' caps of all kinds. The latter may be sold on commission, while all the rest can be solicited.

The Candy Booth will contain home-made candies:

| | |
|---|---|
| Chocolate Creams, | Chocolate Caramels. |
| Cocoanut Creams, | Cocoanut Taffy, |
| Cream Dates, | Cream Figs, |
| Cream Almonds, | Cream Walnuts. |

In this booth may also be sold

| | | |
|---|---|---|
| Apples, | Bananas, | Currants, |
| Apricots, | Citron, | Cranberries. |
| | Cocoanuts. | |

For refreshments, choose from the following:

| | |
|---|---|
| Angels' Food, | Artificial Snow, |
| Ambrosia, | Almond Macaroons, |
| Apple Snow, | Apple Float, |
| Boiled Custard, | Baked Custard, |
| Cinnamon Rolls, | Charlotte Russe, |
| Cookies, | Chocolate Blanc Mange, |
| Caledonian Cream, | Coffee Cake, |
| Chocolate Macaroons, | Chocolate Cake, |
| Cocoanut Cake. | Citron Cake, |

Crackers and Cheese.

| | | | |
|---|---|---|---|
| Chocolate, | Cocoa, | Coffee, | Cream. |

The social may be given by members of a society whose names begin with A, B or C.  A. B. C invitation cards may also be issued.

## Art Exhibition.

All who have not yet done so, will certainly want to hold an Art Exhibition. Shelves are arranged as in a store, on which to display the "pictures." Cover them with cambric or paper. Over the doorway have printed in bright colors, "Art Exhibition."

Or, if preferred, numerous lunch tables with pretty spreads, tastefully arranged, may be used for the display instead of the shelves, and are less trouble.

Have prettily printed catalogues of the "pictures," each picture being numbered. In arranging the "pictures," each one is also numbered and arranged in order, from *one* up. The catalogues may be sold for a trifle, or are given to each guest. In the latter case, charge an admission of twenty-five cents to the exhibition.

Each guest takes his catalogue, and proceeds to examine the rare works of art in the gallery.

The following list of "pictures" with their explanations may be placed on exhibition:

### CATALOGUE.

1. A Study of Fish. (In oil.)
2. A Beauty from the South.
3. The Watch on the Rhine.
4. Saved.
5. The Missing Link.
6. A Bad Spell of Weather.
7. The Light of Other Days.
8. The Peace Makers.
9. A City in Ireland.
10. Out for the Night.
11. More than a Match.
12. View of a Well Known Prison.
13. A Little Indian.
14. Somebody's Darling.

15. Birthplace of Burns.
16. The Wreck.
17. View of Boston.
18. Sweet Sixteen.
19. Mill on the Floss.
20. Something to Adore.
21. A Perfect Foot.
22. Gems of the Emerald Isle.
23. A Popular Belle.
24. The Village Frier.
25. The First Sorrow.
26. The Red Skins.
27. The Sweethearts.
28. Fireside Companions.
29. The Skipper's Home on the Rhine.
30. Rose of Castile.
31. Maid of Orleans.
32. Bonaparte Crossing the Rhine.
33. Declined with Thanks.
34. Cause of the Revolution.
35. Can't be Beat.
36. The Beau and the Belle.
37. A Great Invention.
38. A Swimming Match.
39. A View of Brussels.
40. Our Colored Waiter.
41. The Worn Travellers.
42. A Source of Tears.
43. "All on Board!"
44. Caught in a Squall.
45. Harp of the Israelites.
46. The Seasons.
47. A View of Long Branch.
48. The Evergreen Vale.
49. Flower of the Family.
50. Hands Off!

### EXPLANATIONS.

1. A box of sardines.
2. An orange.

3. A watch on a cheese rind.
4. A child's bank containing money.
5. A chain of sausage with a link missing.
6. "Weather," badly spelled.
7. A Tallow Candle.
8. Scissors.
9. A Cork.
10. A lamp, outened.
11. Half a dozen matches.
12. A rat trap.
13. A small dish of corn meal.
14. A pug dog.
15. A flatiron
16. A worn out umbrella.
17. A hub.
18. Sixteen pieces of candy.
19. A coffee mill setting on some floss.
20. Locks and hinges.
21. A foot rule.
22. Potatoes.
23. The dinner bell.
24. A frying pan.
25. A broken doll.
26. Rosy cheeked apples.
27. Two candy hearts.
28. Poker and Tongs.
29. A piece of cheese rind.
30. Rows of Castile soap.
31. Molasses taffy.
32. A bone, partly across a cheese rind.
33. A poem on "Spring."
34. Tacks on tea.
35. A radish.
36. A bow of ribbon and a dumb bell.
37. A nutmeg grater.
38. A match, floating on the water.
39. A brussels rug.
40. A tray.

41.   An old pair of boots.
42.   An onion.
43.   An awl on a board.
44.   A fish.
45.   A Jew's harp.
46.   A box of pepper and one of salt.
47.   A long branch.
48.   A green veil.
49.   A sack of flour.
50.   An old clock without hands.

### Easter Sale.

Arrangements for an Easter Sale should be completed about a week before Easter—the sale continuing through an afternoon and evening. As so many exchange gifts with their friends at this time, there will be no trouble in disposing of all the pretty articles that can be solicited.

Hand-painted Easter cards, satin panels, banners, palettes, also pieces of hand-painted china are dainty and pretty; also colored eggs, arranged in small fancy baskets, match-safes made of egg-shells fastened together and hung up by narrow ribbons, egg tooth-pick holders, egg cups, white and colored egg "darners," and many other little things, appropriate to the time, will suggest themselves.

In the evening give a program of Easter songs, recitations and readings.

Use potted plants, Easter lilies if possible, for decorating the room where the sale is held.

At six o'clock an "egg supper" is served, the bill of fare being as follows:

| | |
|---|---|
| Egg on toast, | Egg omelet. |
| Ham and eggs, | Poached eggs. |
| Scrambled eggs, | Soft boiled eggs. |

Hard boiled eggs.                    Fried eggs.
Egg custards.                        Egg-nog.
            Rolls, tea and Coffee.

--------  ❖

## Fish Supper.

A pleasing variation from an ordinary bill of fare is a Fish Supper.

Arrange the supper tables in one large room where the evening entertainment is also given, if one is desired.

In the center of the room arrange a fish pond (for ornamentation only) in as realistic a way as possible.

A huge tub of water, surrounded by a bank of greens, with rockery, will answer nicely.

In the pond put several toy boats in which are seated the fishermen. Several toy fishermen may also fish from the banks.

Over the pond suspend an immense pasteboard fish, with the head, tail, and scales outlined with black ink.

Arrange also a tiny fish pond on each supper table. This may be done by using an oval or oblong mirror to represent the water, with moss or vines for the banks; or, an oblong low dish of water, with the banks of green may be used.

Festoons of fish-net may reach from over the central pond to each table, while fish-poles of all sizes, together with fishing tackle, are grouped here and there around the room.

For the supper, choose from the following:

Codfish, on Toast.                   Codfish Balls.
Baked White Fish.                    Canned Salmon.
Smoked Sturgeon.                     Halibut.
Fresh Fish, Fried.                   Broiled Fish.
Mackerel.                            Herring.

Mustard Sardines.            Lobster Salad.
Salmon Salad.              Fish Chowder.

The ladies serving the supper wear fish-net aprons.

There may also be a booth of fishermen's supplies, where the gentlemen will be glad to make their purchases. Have on sale fish-bags of burlap, or canvas, with a fancy design outlined in bright colors, jointed poles, fish hooks and lines, fish baskets, and luminous bait of all kinds.

If there is a program, it should be given by the gentlemen. A dozen or two gentlemen might relate, with perfect accuracy, and in a strictly truthful manner, their "experiences" in fishing—how many caught, the size of same, the secrets of good fishing, the different ways of fishing, etc.

— ❖ — — —

### Peanut Party.

There are several novel ways of giving a Peanut Party, each of which will keep a company of young people active and jolly for the greater part of an evening.

Let the hostess purchase a quantity of peanuts, according to the number of guests expected, and hide them in every available place in the rooms where the guests are to be entertained. In the folds of curtains and draperies, behind doors and pictures, in vases, under mats and chairs, on the mantel or cabinet, in the foliage of plants, *everywhere.*

Make, like shopping bags, as many pretty little bags of various colors of cheese-cloth or silk as there are guests expected.

The bags may be plain, or if of silk, they have a design of peanuts, outlined or painted upon one side.

After all the guests have arrived, a bag is given to each, with instructions to fill it as soon as possible.

The one who is through first is presented with a handsome hand-painted satchet bag.

If the party is given for amusement only, each guest keeps his bag when filled. If for the purpose of raising money, they are sold for five or ten cents each.

Here is another way:—Provide as many tinted cards as guests are expected—pink for the ladies and cream for the gentlemen.

Separate lengthwise a peanut, take out the kernel, and fasten one half of the shell to a pink card, the other to the cream. Proceed in this way till all the cards are supplied. Use peanuts of all sizes from the largest to the smallest and of odd shapes.

Each guest selects a card and matches the shell, with that on one of the cards of contrasting color. After all the shells are matched, the company is seated at supper.

---

### Valentine Party.

An old-time and pretty custom, especially among Southern people, is the giving of Valentine Parties on St. Valentine eve. Nearly all young people and many older ones, are more or less interested in the observance of the day, and in no prettier way can it be observed than by giving a Valentine Party.

Let the ladies, young and old, of a society, issue written or printed invitations to an equal number of gentlemen to attend. State upon invitation that the ladies will wear special costumes for the occasion, and that each gentleman will receive a valentine, providing he will recite a verse of poetry suitable to the day, to the lady presenting the valentine to him. Each lady dresses in fancy costume and represents a valentine—either "comic" or "pretty." The characters from Shakespeare and Dickens are good, also Greenaway, Chinese and Japanese costumes. Martha Washington, Joan of Arc, Queen Bess, and others as they are thought of, may be represented. Some good comic costumes will be easily planned, and just in place.

Each lady must also make a pretty valentine, or souvenir, either a hand-decorated valentine, or a pretty little fancy article that a gentleman would appreciate. A pen-wiper (there are many pretty kinds), a courtplaster case, stamp case, a match safe, or a pretty satchet would all be very acceptable. Each lady will also enclose her visiting card in an envelope, and seal it.

On the evening of the party, the sealed envelopes are indiscriminately thrown into a fancy basket and placed on a table in a prominent part of the room.

After the gentlemen arrive and greetings have been exchanged, let the company be seated.

A paper or talk on "St. Valentine's Day," is then given by one of the ladies. She speaks of the origin and customs of the day, the meaning of valentines, the sending of gifts, the different kinds of valentines, and the four classes of people to whom they are sent friends, lovers, children and enemies. At the close of her talk she invites the gentlemen to come forward, one by one, as she calls their names. As each one comes, he takes one of the envelopes out of the basket, opens it, and announces the name of the lady whose card he finds. She then comes forward and asks him what message he brings of St. Valentine's day. He repeats his verse and she presents him with the souvenir she has provided- He, in turn, may if he wishes present her with a bunch of flowers or a box of bon-bons.

Later on, warm maple sugar, or hickory nuts and pop-corn may be served. Instead of charging for refreshments, serve them to all, and let it be understood that each one, as he leaves the refreshment room, may leave a voluntary offering. Larger sums are sometimes realized in this way, than by having a fixed price.

---  ✧

### Children's Fair.

The Childrens' Fair is one of the most interesting and profitable entertainments that can be given. It is similar to, and conducted much the same as a county fair, and may be continued through several days and evenings.

Let a number of ladies having the fair in charge, extend an invitation to all children under fifteen years of age, to meet them at a certain time and place.

A full and clear explanation of what the fair is to be, must be made to them and their enthusiasm will be aroused. Several hundred children can easily be interested, each of whom will have from one to half a dozen articles to exhibit. Any boy or girl, under fifteen years of age, may enter any article or articles, of his own handiwork, or in his own pos-session. If children wish, they may donate the articles, in which case they are sold on the last evening of the fair, otherwise they are returned to the exhibitor.

If pains are taken to interest the children, the results of their efforts will be surprising. There will be doll's dresses, aprons, bonnets, paper flowers, tidies, cushions, knitted and crocheted lace, patchwork, pies, cakes, bread, painting and drawing, charcoal work, engines, tops, modelling in clay, kindergarten work, wood carving, and other things without number.

These articles must all be classified by the ladies in charge.

Arrange a number of booths for the various departments Domestic, Floral, Mechanical, Art, Culinary, etc., and place each article to be exhibited, in its proper department.

Three judges (ladies and gentlemen) must be appointed for each department, and must award first and second premiums. Fifty cents for a first, and twenty-five cents for a second premium are suitable amounts, and will show an appreciation of the children's efforts.

A nice way to award them is to procure bright, new coins, and put each in a little pasteboard box, lined with pink cotton, such as jewellers use, writing on the lid of the box the name of the child to whom the premium is given. Appoint a person to publicly award the premiums on the last evening of the fair, also to sell all articles that have been donated.

The fair should be open each day, as well as in the evening.

Dinners may also be served by the ladies.

This will attract many parents and friends who would not otherwise come.

Each evening a children's program is given, and a light lunch may be served by them under the direction of the ladies.

Dinner tickets, which also admit to the fair, also admission tickets to the fair only, and "season" tickets for dinners, fair and lunch, should be previously printed and put in the hands of the children to sell.

Prices may be as follows:

Dinner tickets        -        -        -        -        -        25 cents each
Admission to fair        -        -        -        -        -        10 cents
Admission to fair and lunch        -        -        -        -        -        20 cents
" Season" tickets, including two dinners and lunches,
            and admission to fair        -        -        -        One dollar

## Parlor Entertainment.

Charades, and tableaux together with a few games constitute this entertainment.  Large double parlors, with
portieres between, are needed, using one room for the guests,
the other for those who take part.

An admission is charged at the door, and refreshments
are served in a side room after the evening's entertainment—
an extra charge being made for them.

For charades, the following list of words will be found
helpful :

| | |
|---|---|
| Gal-vest-on, | U-ni-vers-al, |
| In-vest-i-gate, | Met-ro-pol-i-tan, |
| Bal-ti-more, | Dic-tion-ary, |
| Par-a-lyze, | Ges-tic-u-late, |
| Massa-chu-setts, | Syn-tax, |
| O-hi-o, | Sub-ju-gate, |
| Chrys-an-the-mum, | Met-e-or-o-log-i-cal, |
| Miles-Stan-dish, | In-com-pre-hen-si-bil-i-ty, |
| Pres-by-ter-i-an, | Ad-just-able, |

Analyze,        [Anna reclines.]
Matrimony,        [Matter-'o-money.]
Cauliflower,        [Call "Rose" or "Daisy."]

If tableaux are given the following are good and do not
require much preparation :

| | |
|---|---|
| "Maud Muller," | "Morning and Night," |
| "Love's Young Dream," | "The Dreamers," |
| "Grecian Maidens," | "Evangeline," |
| "Single Blessedness," | "Spring," |
| "Summer,"        "Autumn," | "Winter." |

"Aurora Leigh."
> " I'm thinking how 'twas morning then;
> And now 'tis night."

"Priscilla."
> " The form of the maiden Priscilla,
> Seated beside her wheel,
> And the carded wool like a snowdrift
> Piled at her knee,
> Her white hands feeding
> The ravenous spindles."

> "Beautiful Isle of the Sea—
> Thy memory is precious to me."

[A huge bottle labled "Cod Liver Oil "]

> "May has come ;
> Gentle, delicate footed May
> With all her wealth of green."

[A little girl—"May"—in tattered dress and sunbonnet, wearing large, coarse shoes, an immense basket of "greens" on her arm.]

Character readings and recitations may be given and games should be provided for those who care for them.

Several games that all can play are as follows :

Between the sliding doors leave just enough space for a face to appear. Let one of the players drape a black shawl over his head and shoulders leaving only the eyes uncovered. He then appears in the doorway, and the players are to guess who he is. Or, the eyes and forehead may be hidden, leaving the nose and mouth exposed.

The "coquette's game" is as follows : One of the young ladies is asked to name half a dozen of her favorite flowers. She mentions the lily, daisy, pansy, mignonette, heliotrope and carnation.

She then leaves the room and six of the party are then given the same names. She is then called back and is asked. "What do you think of the rose?" She may answer, "It is always lovely!" "What will you do with the heliotrope?" Perhaps she will say, "I'll set it aside when its beauty is gone." "What will you do with the pansy?" "I'll cherish it kindly, always."

She may thus find, when told whom they represent, that she has promised to cherish the one who is indifferent to her, and that she has "cast aside" her dearest friend.

Shadow pictures also afford unlimited fun.

Across the doorway of a small room adjoining the parlor, stretch a sheet. In the back part of the room place a light

The lights in the parlor are lowered. The players then appear in turn behind the sheet in comic costumes and attitudes and the guests are to guess who they are.

## The District School.

If nicely planned and carried out, any amount of amusement is afforded by holding a session of the District School.

Select a gentleman, very familiar with the old-time district school to act as schoolmaster. He will wear a spike-tailed coat, knee breeches, low shoes with buckles, and a powdered wig Several dozen scholars are also dressed in old-fashioned costumes and assume old-fashioned names.

The stage is arranged as an old-time school room, with desks and benches, and curtains must be used.

Divide the time to represent the morning session, nooning, and the afternoon session.

In the morning the teacher calls the roll, which is responded to by "here" or "present, sir." Some of the scholars volunteer excuses for absent pupils, which are very amusing and rather uncomplimentary. One tardy pupil, to escape merited punishment, presents the teacher with an immense head of cabbage.

Next comes a singing exercise, with motions to imitate washing the face, combing the hair, milking the cow, sweeping the room, etc.

The spelling class is now called, and made to toe the mark, and to wrestle with such words as "phthisic" and "cachinnation," the teacher calling out "next" as each word is missed, the pupil who spells it correctly going to the "head."

The efforts of the lisping girl and the stuttering boy, in their attempts at spelling, will bring down the house.

After this class is dismissed, the geography class is called, and come forward, being seated on a long bench in front of the teacher's desk. This class, unfortunately, is not well prepared. The teacher asks " What state has two capitals?" Dull boy answers " New York." " Name them." "Capital N, and Capital Y."

Others, eager to answer, snap their fingers to gain attention.

The teacher is here interrupted by a girl who comes forward with her slate and asks aid in solving the following problem: If one dozen eggs are taken out of a basket, how many are left? He looks at her in a puzzled way, scratches his head, gives it up, and sends her to her seat. The teacher now asks " In what state is Boston?" No one seems ever to have heard of such a place, and after venturing numerous answers, as, "Ohio," "California" or " Indiana," they are sent to their seats in disgrace.

The grammar class comes next, parsing "grass" as a verb, "who" as a noun, "run" as an adjective, etc., after which the morning session is dismissed.

While the stage is being arranged for "nooning," let one of the scholars give a comic song, or a recitation.

The scene at noon is now presented. The girls are seated in groups on one side of the room, opening pails and baskets containing lunch, while the boys are on the other side.

As the lunch proceeds, they chat, tell stories, and exchange with each other a part of the contents of their lunch baskets. Some have pumpkin pie, cake, bottles of milk and coffee, while others have pieces of sausage, baked beans, sandwiches, hard boiled eggs and corn bread.

After lunch, the girls play "ring round a rosy" and "little Sally Watters." The boys sit astride the benches and play "mumblety peg," or carve their initials on the desks, occasionally casting sly glances at the girls.

Next comes the afternoon session, when the district committee is expected, and teacher and scholars appear in their "Sunday best," the latter having been repeatedly warned to do their best, as an "exhibition" was to be given.

Presently Deacon Jones and Squire Ancient appear in old-time costume, and are given seats by the teacher's desk. They partake freely of tobacco and snuff. The exercises now begin. Arabella Tomkinson delivers the "address of welcome," to which Deacon Jones responds.

Maria Millikens follows with an essay on "Spring." The reading class, having been previously drilled, is now called, and each one tries to outdo the other, in reading the different verses of "Marco Bozzaris."

The next exercise is a declamation by Jonathan Wilkins entitled "Make Way for Liberty." This is very impressive, Jonathan's gestures and (lack of) enthusiasm throughout making it very interesting.

During this effort at oratory Squire Ancient falls asleep and the bad boy steals up and pins a slip of paper on his back. This act, however, does not escape the eye of Deacon Jones, who looks reproachfully at the teacher, who in turn gets his whip. Jerusha Jenkins now asks permission to "pass the water;" also tells on Hezekiah Billman, who is making faces at Sally Miller.

Elizabeth Williams recites, with great simplicity, "Twinkle, twinkle, little star," and Andrew Johnson reads an essay on "Girls."

The school now sings the multiplication table and the teacher calls on Squire Ancient for remarks. The latter rises, deliberately removes his spectacles, and proceeds *not* to congratulate the teacher and scholars on the success of the afternoon's program, but instead, to find fault with the teacher's "new fangled notions," such as omitting the "rule of three" and leaving the k out of "musick." He also severely reprimands him for his lack of government. The teacher looks about uneasily, and turns pale while the 'Squire proceeds to state that they will have to "turn him out." At hearing this, the school bursts into tears and sings "Auld Lang Syne," and school is dismissed.

---

### Leaf Social.

This entertainment is prettiest in the fall, when the leaves are turning—the autumn leaves making more showy decorations.

Use nothing but leaves and vines for decorating.

Festoons of leaves, strung on twine, are showy and pretty; also large branches of forest trees on which the leaves are turned.

Woodbine, just coloring, is especially pretty. If refreshments are served, have vases of bright colored leaves on the tables.

A central table, elaborately decorated with leaves, in fancy designs, adds much to the effect of the supper room. At each plate, just at the edge of the napkin, place a bright autumn leaf, waxed and pressed. Leaf shaped programs cut out of colored bristol board,'or out of white card board, and "veined" with colored ink, are very pretty, and a pleasure to make.

At the entrance is placed a stand on which a leaf shaped dish is placed, with the notice on a leaf shaped card, ;"Leave your Dime."

Following is the program :

Music - - - - - - - - Leaves from Beethoven
Original Miscellany - - - - - - "Stray Leaves"
Recitation - - - - - - A leaf from one of the poets
Paper - - - - - - - - "Autumn Leaves"
Music - - - - - - - "Leaf by Leaf the Roses Fall"

### Dairy Maid's Lunch.

A Dairy Maid's Lunch is given in a large hall or room where different apartments in which to serve refreshments can be arranged.

A large modern attic is one of the best of places.

Every young lady who assists with the lunch, or in any way, should wear a dairy maid's costume.

One made as follows is inexpensive and pretty: A full skirt of cream and red striped print, full gathered waist of cream cheese cloth, having gathered elbow sleeves with frill, and black velvet girdle. A cap of white lace or cheese cloth is also worn, and low shoes or slippers.

Another costume is of indigo blue print, full straight skirt and tight waist, white apron, cap, and neckerchief.

The costumes may be uniform or each may choose a different material and style.

The former is preferable, especially if a march or drill precedes the serving of the lunch.

An informal reception might also be held before lunch.

Following is the bill of fare:

| | |
|---|---|
| Bread and milk - - - - - - | 10 cents |
| Baked apples and milk - - - - | 10 cents |
| Mush and milk - - - - - - | 10 cents |
| Crackers and milk - - - - - - | 10 cents |
| Milk, per glass - - - - - - | 5 cents |
| Fresh butter milk - - - - - | 5 cents |
| Cottage cheese - - - - - - | 5 cents |
| Crackers and cheese - - - - - | 5 cents |

Bread and milk, and crackers and milk, may be served in one booth. Baked apples and milk, and mush and milk in another, milk and buttermilk in another, and crackers and cheese, and cottage cheese in another. Gingerbread and milk, also pumpkin pie, may be added to the bill of fare.

The guests go from one booth to another, being served to what they wish, the lady in charge of each booth giving them checks for the amounts purchased in her booth. Have one cashier for the evening. Milk stools, pails and churns may be on sale, also fresh butter, cheese by the pound, cottage cheese and cream.

---:.:---

### Jean Ingelow Evening.

A Jean Ingelow Evening has been twice observed by a large and flourishing church, having been very successful each time.

The following program was given, the prominent feature being the "The Songs of Seven."

Solo (Song Folio) "O Fair Dove, O Fond Dove."
Paper "Jean Ingelow."
Recitation "The High Tide."
Song (Song Folio) "On the Rocks by Aberdeen."
"Songs of Seven" Exultation, Romance, Love, Maternity, Widowhood, Giving in Marriage, Longing for Home.

For the Songs of Seven there should be a prettily arranged garden scene, which, with little change, can be used for each of the seven parts. Arrange, on the platform, several rustic chairs and benches, and a garden vase and hammock. Also potted plants and branches of trees or evergreens. Several singing birds, in pretty cages, will also add to the effect.

"Seven Times One" should be a bright little girl, dressed in white, who trips lightly upon the platform "jumping the rope," and then recites her part as though she were proud to say

"I am seven times one to-day."

"Seven Times Two" now appears upon the platform a school girl, carrying an armful of books and her sun-hat. She lays aside her books, sits carelessly down and recites her part—"Romance."

"Seven Times Three" is a sweet young lady, prettily dressed, waiting for her lover. The lights are lowered during this recitation.

"I leaned out of window, I smelled the white clover-
Dark, dark was the garden—I saw not the gate."

For "Seven Times Four" the lights are again turned up. The mother is seated in a rocker, humming a tune, a piece of needlework in her hands, when the "lads and lassies" run in with their daisies, buttercups and daffodils, for "mother to thread them a daisy chain."

The lights are now lowered for "Seven Times Five" a widow walking slowly about in the garden—then seating herself in a chair—her arm leaning on the arm of the chair, and her hands folded, she recites her poem—"Widowhood."

In "Seven Times Six" the mother and daughter appear together upon the platform, the mother in a handsome dark dress, the daughter in bridal array.

> "To hear, to heed, to wed,
> Fair lot that maidens choose."

Just after the mother's recitation have a tableau to represent the marriage—a full bridal scene.

In "Seven Times Seven" an old lady with neckerchief and cap walks slowly upon the platform and, leaning upon her cane, recites "Longings for Home."

> "I pray you, what is that nest to me—
> My empty nest!

In choosing those to represent the several parts, choose those who are specially adapted to the parts, and the results of the entertainment will be more than satisfactory.

The poems will all be found in any complete copy of Jean Ingelow's works.

### Cobweb Party.

"Weave" a cobweb of strong twine throughout the rooms (upstairs and down) hall, passage ways, and stairs of a large house.

The more you tangle it the better (or worse) for the guests whose duty it will be to unravel it.

After guests have arrived, and greetings have been exchanged, the hostess instructs each to take from a tray a numbered card—the ladies from one tray—the gentlemen from another. To each one she also gives a small stick, on which to wind the twine. The twines for the ladies to wind begin at one place—say the library table; those for the gentlemen at another. At the end of each twine is a numbered card, and each guest selects the one corresponding with the number already held and begins to wind, following wherever the twine leads, out and in, back and forth, up and down, sometimes getting knotted up with somebody else's twine, wondering if you will ever reach the end, and whether the house will ever be restored to order.

Finally, after many difficulties and trials of patience, and numerous "collisions," the end is reached, when, if she wishes, the hostess may place a cobweb with its occupant, (such as are used for fancy work,) which each guest will keep as a souvenir.

Supper is then announced, after which an outline of the evening's experiences may be given by the guests.

— ❖

### Antique Reception and Tea.

All maids and matrons participating in this entertainment wear costumes of "ye olden time."

A large hall, with open fireplace, is the best place in which to give it. In the fireplace have the andirons, kettle, etc., with strings of dried apples hung on either side.

In one corner have a large, old fashioned clock, in another, a spinning wheel with a maid at work, and in another a "dasher" churn. Old-fashioned chairs and other articles of furniture are placed here and there about the room. The rifle hangs over the door, and an old-fashioned couch. with calico curtains and blue counterpane sets near the fireplace.

Bunches of asparagus hung upon the walls over old-time pictures, or suspended from the ceiling, will add to the antique effect of the room.

In the middle of the room are spread long tables, plainly furnished with old linen and china. Benches are placed at the tables instead of chairs, and a simple old-time bill of fare is served  The room and tables are lighted entirely by candles in brass candle-sticks.

At the end of each table place a pail of water, with a gourd to drink from.

Instead of having a program, substitute a "spelling bee" or a "singing school."

## Children's Jubilee.

Children usually feel more interest and responsibility in the success of their entertainments than older persons do in theirs.

The Children's Jubilee is best given in the summer, when flowers are plentiful. though tissue paper flowers can be substituted nicely.

Each girl represents a flower. and each boy a bird or insect. The girls should all dress in white. wearing upon the head a wreath of the flowers they choose to represent, and should carry a bunch of same in the hand.

One girl chooses the rose  wearing a wreath of roses. and recites a verse or poem on "The Rose." Another chooses the morning-glory or the nasturtium. has her dress festooned with vines of same, and recites a verse or sings a song to represent her flower. Others choose the dandelion, lily, violet, pansy, sunflower, daisy, goldenrod, buttercup, bluebell, red clover, daffodil, mignonette or marigold, each reciting a verse or singing a song.

Each boy represents a bird the lark, bobolink, whip-poor-will, robin, woodpecker, canary, etc., or an insect— the grasshopper, beetle, butterfly, bumblebee or hornet, and recites a poem to represent the same.

All of the children's magazines of the day abound in short and witty poems, songs and stories, about flowers, birds and insects, so that no difficulty need be experienced in finding something appropriate for each thing represented.

Several choruses of "flowers" and "birds" will complete the program.

After the program, the girls may have a flower sale, and the boys a candy and lemonade stand, or a lunch may be served by the boys and girls.

Have printed programs arranged something like this:

| | |
|---|---|
| Chorus | By the Birds and Flowers |
| Recitation | By the Violet |
| Song | By Robin Redbreast |
| My History | The Morning Glory |

Follow this out during the entire program, using no names except those of the birds and flowers.

The entertainment is very interesting to the children themselves, and delightful to all.

-- - --❖

### Conundrum Social.

At a Conundrum Social each gentleman is given a numbered card, on which a conundrum is written. Each lady is also given a numbered card on which the answer is written.

The leader, or hostess, calls on No. 1 to read his conundrum. Each guest guesses at the answer, and if no one guesses correctly the lady holding the answer to No. 1 reads it. No. 2 is then called, and so on, till all have been given.

When supper is announced, each gentleman will escort the lady to supper, whose number corresponds with his own.

Menu cards must be provided, containing the menu in conundrums only, while the ladies serving same must be very familiar with the interpretations.

If any guest is able to interpret the entire menu he is presented with a handsome book.

### MENU.

| | | |
|---|---|---|
| The Poor Man's Staff | - | [Bread]. |
| Food of the Spinning Wheel, | - | [Rolls]. |
| What the Street Cars do on the Switch | - | [Meat]. |
| The Tribe of Ham was Bred there and Mustered | - | [Sandwiches]. |
| Causes of Neighborhood Contention | - | [Chickens]. |
| Most Delightful Age of Childhood | - | [Sauce-age]. |
| An Unruly Member | - | [Tongue]. |
| I've Been Basted, Now I'm Baked | - | [Turkey]. |
| The Irishman's Toes | - | [Potatoes]. |
| I Come from Under the Rhine | - | [Cheese]. |
| My Mother Makes Me Sharp | - | [Vinegar]. |
| Tabby's Party | - | [Cats-up]. |
| Hidden Tears | - | [Onions]. |
| I Feel It from My Heart | - | [Beets]. |
| I'm Sour, but You'll Like Me, | - | [Pickles]. |
| The Heathen Chinee, | - | [Chow-chow]. |
| Congealed Noise | - | [Ice-cream]. |
| Changeable Politicians | - | [Turn-overs]. |
| Something to Take | - | [Cake]. |
| Musical Cake | - | [Do-nuts]. |
| Impertinence | - | [Sauce]. |
| The Bugbear of History | - | [Dates]. |
| Stale Jokes | - | [Chestnuts]. |
| Fruit of the Vine | - | [Grapes]. |
| I Settled Just Above Ground | - | [Coffee]. |
| Old Maid's Letter, or Boston Overthrow | - | [Tea]. |
| Spring Offerings | - | [Water]. |

## The Bell Social.

Bell-shaped programs or cards of invitation are provided for this social.

Each young lady participating dresses to represent a "belle," either modern or ancient.

There will be the city belle, the village belle, the country belle, the modern belle, and the belle of fifty years ago.

The following program may be given, in addition to which have several choruses with a "ringing movement," the singers keeping time to the music with tea bells of various sizes and tones.

Chorus.
Essay—"Bells."
Recitation—"The Belfry Pigeon."
Essay—"Belles."
Recitation—"The Modern Belle."
Reading—"The Bells."
Recitation—"Seven Times Two."
Chorus.

During the reading—"The Bells," let a number of persons, out of sight, keep time with bells, suited in tone to each verse, at the proper place, as,

"Hear the sledges with the bells,
   *Silver bells!*"

"How they *tinkle, tinkle, tinkle.*"

"Hear the *mellow* wedding bells,
   *Golden Bells!*"

"Hear the *loud alarum* bells,
   *Brazen bells!*"

"Hear the *tolling* of the bells,
   *Iron Bells!*"

The recitations mentioned may be found in Bryant's "Library of Poetry and Song."

If properly understood and thoroughly practiced, the effect of the bells in the choruses, and in the reading is delightful.

After the program, the *tea bell* announces that the *belles* are ready to serve a dainty lunch. A tiny bell, such as are used for fancy work, tied with a blue or pink ribbon, is given to each guest at the supper table.

------------:------------

### Bird Concert.

A Bird Concert is given by fifty or one hundred girls and boys, not over twelve years of age, and all the songs, and recitations, if any, must pertain to birds. For the choruses, much thorough drilling is necessary, as the children must sing without music or copies of words.

The following songs from the "Song Cabinet," are specially pretty and easy to learn:

> "The Spring Bird,"
> "I Wish I Were a Birdie,"
> "The Boy and the Bobolink,"
> "The Bobolink's Reply,"
> "The Bird Carol,"
> "Death of the Robin,"
> "The Birds' Ball,"
> "Song of the Bobolink."

In addition to the choruses, have several solos and duets by the "wee ones," also three or four nice recitations.

Arranged about the platform have a number of singing birds in gilt cages. Their singing, sometimes during the solos and recitations is very amusing to the children.

Charge an admission of fifteen cents, and give to each child from ten to twenty-five tickets to sell, keeping a careful account of same.

Each one will thus feel a personal responsibility and interest, and a large audience is assured. Solicit advertisements for the programs and thus defray expense of same.

The children pass the programs on the evening of the concert.

———◦———

### May Day Greeting.

This entertainment should be given in a large hall, with a spacious platform at one end.

Two prominent features of the program are the winding of the Maypole and the reading of Tennyson's "May Queen," with tableaux.

Have a number of Mayday choruses, recitations and songs, while for the opening number have Milton's "May Morning" recited, with a tableau to represent

"The flowery May, who from her green lap throws
The yellow cowslip and the pale primrose."

All the girls taking part in the winding of the Maypole, or singing in the choruses, are dressed in white, with wreaths of flowers on the head. A march during the singing of one of the choruses is pretty. For the winding of the Maypole they must have repeated practice, a number of pretty movements being introduced.

During the reading of the "May Queen," have tableaux as follows:

1. Alice with "knots of flowers and buds and garlands gay."

2. "Robin leaning on the bridge."

3. "Beneath the hawthorn on the grass
They made me Queen of May * * *
And we danced about the Maypole
And in the hazel copse."

4. "Oh! Blessings on his kindly heart,
And on his silver hair!" * * *

A thousand times I blest him as
He knelt beside my bed."

5.   " But sit beside my bed, mother,
And put your hand in mine—
And Effie on the other side,
And I will tell the sign."

The tableaux are one of the prettiest features of the entertainment. If plenty of flowers cannot be had, use part paper, or other artificial flowers.

The entertainment is best given in the afternoon—perhaps on Saturday. when young people are at leisure to attend.

### Flower Sale.

A Flower Sale is held early in the spring when plants are needed for bedding.

Plants may either be solicited, or procured of a florist and sold on commission. Booths are arranged and prettily trimmed for the different varieties—geraniums in one. roses in another, and so on. A central booth should be made specially attractive and contains baskets of cut flowers, and hand and button-hole bouquets.

Bunches of paper flowers, now so beautifully made, will find ready sale and will add materially to the proceeds.

Another booth contains large and small pieces of satin, plush or velvet, on which are handsomely painted or embroidered sprays of flowers—these to be sold and made into fancy work. Any article of fancy work, or piece of china decorated in a similar manner, is appropriate and salable. Flowered scrims and cretonnes may be made into useful and fancy articles, and sold.

A reception committee, consisting of a flower girl from

each booth, will add to the comfort and pleasure of the guests, and each member of said committee may act as a representative for her booth.

A little corner might be reserved for packages of flower seeds, either home-grown, or procured of a florist, to be sold at five and ten cents each.

Books on the culture and care of flowers may also be on sale.

———— ❖ —— - -

### " S " Supper and Social.

The above named entertainment was recently given in one of the large Southern cities and was unique and attractive. Have menu cards printed as follows:

### " S " SUPPER.

SUMPTUOUS! SUPERB!! SATISFYING!!!

SUPPER SCHEDULE.

Substantial Soup. '

Slender Slices Turkey, Seasoned with Sage. Steak.

Slimly Sliced Sandwiches, Stylishly Shaped.

Salt Risings, Scantily Sweetened. Sanitary Staff of Life.

Splendid Salmon Salad.

Slaw. S(C)elery.

Sharply Spiced, Slender, Sweet Pickles.

Stimulative Sauce. Sour Pickles.

SWEETS.

Silver Cake. Spice Cake. Sponge Cake. Snowballs.

SIPS.

Sister's Special Steeped Sip. Steaming Satisfying Stimulant.

————

SUPPER—Six to Seven.

Seventeen Sedate Sisters Serve Supper.

ADMISSION— Several Shillings.

Small Sale of Seasonable Articles.

The sale may be held in the afternoon and after supper, while later in the evening a program is given as follows:

Sweet Song.
Short Story.
Several Spicy Speeches.
Selections from a Stray Scrap-book.
Suggestions for Self-support.
String Solo.
Song by a Sextette.

The invitations should be printed on a pasteboard letter "S," the menu cards being separate.

--------:--------

### Yesterday and To-day Reception.

Arrange two apartments, one to represent "yesterday," the other "to-day." In the middle of each apartment arrange the supper table.

Those of yesterday are as antique as possible, with old china and glass, and old-fashioned table linen. The tables in this room are lighted with tallow candles in brass candle-sticks. Scattered about the room have old rockers and "settees," and old-fashioned braided rugs upon the floor.

A bill of fare of "yesterday" is served by old-fashioned girls of all ages. Serve the following: Baked beans, corn bread, mince and pumpkin pie, gingerbread, seed cakes and "twisted" doughnuts.

In the room representing "to-day" have several elegantly furnished dining tables, with several smaller lunch tables Use plenty of silver, glass and china, also fruit and flower pieces.

Modern girls will serve supper, consisting of escalloped oysters, oyster patties, chicken and lobster salad, olives, salted almonds, angel food, ices and ice-cream, and cake, macaroons, etc.

Handsome rugs and art squares are upon the floor. Gas, or large stand and banquet lamps, light the room.

Here and there is an etching, handsomely framed, upon an easel. Bits of bric-a-brac, and a few pieces of modern furniture, complete the room.

Charge twenty-five cents for supper in either room.

——— ✤

### Baby Party.

Invitations to a Baby Party are issued by a two-year-old, to any number of his two-year-old friends. Mothers are invited to come as escorts, and the party is held from three to five o'clock in the afternoon.

Prizes are given the babies as follows, with corresponding burlesque prizes:

To the baby who weighs most.

To the baby who cries least.

To the baby who has the most teeth.

The prize to the one who weighs most is a pair of boots, with a card bearing the following:

"Such a big boy—dear me suz!
Must wear boots like papa does!"

The burlesque prize to the one who weighs least is a package of farina, on which is written:

"Farina mush—not cake and pie
Will make baby grow high as the sky."

The one who cries least is given a silver(?) medal inscribed:

"Model Boy. Oct. , 18–."

The one who cries most is given a bottle of paregoric.

"Don't forget to say 'Thank you!' for it,
For many a pain's cured by paregoric."

To the baby having the largest number of teeth is given a box of tooth-picks, with this timely advice:

"Pick 'em clean, little one,
It will save you a snug sum."

The baby having the least number of teeth is given a rubber ring. with this comfort:

> "If the "toofies" will not come.
> Just you use your little gums."

Lunch tables are now spread. with a bowl of cut flowers and two lighted candles on each.   Two mothers and two babies are seated at each table.

" Good-byes" are then said and the babies go back to their everyday joys and trials.

--- --- ---

### Holiday Fair.

No time of year is more favorable for the successful holding of a fair. than that preceding the Christmas holidays.

The work of preparation is such that it seems wise to continue a fair through several days and evenings. serving dinners and lunches each day.

For the dinners, which if wisely planned are a sure and business like way to increase the proceeds. thorough and systematic preparation must be made.   Tickets should also be sold in advance.

The following booths would be attractive and sure of being well patronized: The "Candy Kitchen." "The Dairy." "The Art Gallery," "The Children's Corner," "Santa Claus' Storehouse." "The Domestic Booth." "Flower Booth." "Country Store." "Lemonade and Ice cream Booth." "Lunch Counter." "The Tea Room." "The Paper Booth." "The Fruit Market." and the "China Booth."

As many are at a loss to know what to make for a fair. the following list of articles is suggested.   Remember that medium and low-priced articles will find more ready sale than high priced articles.   Aprons, sweeping caps, knitted slippers, holders of all kinds, satchet bags, pen wipers, pin cushions, throws, letter holders, watch cases, calendars, useful and fancy bags of all kinds, thermometer cases, towel holders, doylies, postal card cases, stamp cases, cases for visiting cards, court-plaster cases, handkerchief and glove cases, decorated china, charcoal, oil and water-color pictures, drawn linen work, crotcheted hoods, mittens, and fascinators.

In arranging for a fair, a good way to create an interest is to have a "Thimble Party." several weeks or a month in advance.

Invite all the ladies of the society to come together of an afternoon, each bringing materials for the article she wishes to donate. All will thus begin work together. Each will be anxious to do her best, new ideas will be gained, and the more salable articles can be duplicated.

Gentlemen will be invited to tea for which all will pay a small sum. This will create a fund toward the incidental expenses of the fair.

Let children be invited to assist by contributing such articles as they can make. They may also be in charge of the "Children's Corner."

An entertainment should be given each evening—a magic lantern, a "chalk talk," a debate on one of the leading questions of the day, or an entertainment by the children would be enjoyable.

Make the hall as attractive as possible. Use festoons of evergreen, cheese-cloth, or tissue paper, or other inexpensive materials.

Very little money need be spent in conducting a fair—the chief elements of success being *enthusiasm, unity of purpose*, and *hard work*.

### Scotch Social.

This social is given by a score or more of young ladies in Scotch lassie costumes, assisted by half a dozen Scotch lads not over six or eight years old.

For the dresses and shoulder sashes worn by the girls, the domestic ginghams which can now be had in Scotch plaids will answer every purpose and can be used afterward.

The lads will act as ushers, and each is afterward given a tray of home-made *butter-scotch* to sell. The first number of the program is also given by them, for which they must be carefully drilled, so as to be able to sing without words or music.

For the evening's entertainment give a "Burns' program" as follows:

Chorus of Lads—"Auld Lang Syne."
Paper—The Life of Burns.
Recitation—"For A' That, and A' That."
Recitation—"Duncan Gray Cam' Here to Woo."
Reading—"Cotter's Saturday Night."
Recitation—"Auld Robin Gray."
Song—"We'd Better Bide a Wee."

After the program a Scotch bill of fare is served, consisting of oat cakes, porridge, Scotch marmalade, cheese, etc.

An admission of fifteen cents is charged for program and lunch, the butter-scotch being extra.

———— ⋅❖⋅ ——

### Fagot Party.

When the summer vacations are over and everybody has returned home, a pleasant way of meeting together or of entertaining a company is to give a Fagot Party

Invite each guest to "bring a fagot (consisting of a small bundle of sticks) and give a short account of his summer's outing." Some have been to the seashore or moun-

tains, others to one of the numerous summer schools, or
fashionable resorts, while still others have taken overland
trips, or spent a quiet time in the country.    Possibly no two
have visited the same places.

An outline of the route taken, points of interest on the
way, course of reading or study pursued, noted persons
heard or met, accounts of yachting, bathing, mountain
climbing, and many other haps and mishaps, will be a novel
way of entertaining a company and filling an evening with
fun and profit.  Each guest, as his name is called, will throw
his fagot in the open fireplace and relate his experience
while it burns.

A pretty feature, where one gives a "housewarming,"
is to ask each guest to bring a fagot, and as it burns, kind
thoughts and good wishes for the host and hostess may be
expressed.

This feature was recently observed at the "housewarming" of one of the most beautiful mansions in a flourishing
city, many persons of culture and distinction assisting in this
way.

❖

## Bag Sale.

A seasonable time for a Bag Sale is near the holidays,
when one is in search of novel and pretty remembrances for
friends, or just before spring or fall housecleaning, when
every lady likes new things, useful and ornamental, with
which to "freshen up" her home.

There is scarcely a limit to the kinds, sizes and qualities,
nearly every one of which can be put to use in almost any
home.

Have a large number of bags on sale, from the cheapest
to the daintiest and most costly.  When all that have been

donated are brought in, sort them.    Put those for children
together.    Also have a separate place for shopping bags,
satchet bags, stocking bags, etc., with a lady to preside over
each.

Children might have on sale marble bags, school bags,
emory bags, etc.    The bag sale may be held in the afternoon and evening, serving lunch or supper.

In the evening have bag races for the young folks, and
other games.

Have on sale on neatly arranged tables or in booths,
bags of candy, nuts, popcorn, taffy, fruit and bonbons.

A donation of articles worth ten cents may be asked,
each article put in a bag and sold, no one knowing just what
he has purchased till the bag is opened.

Have on sale also a lot of plain and fancy bags of all
sizes, such as grocers and confectioners use.    These are so
often needed in every home, and will sell rapidly.

To those intending to give a bag sale, the following lists
of the various kinds, and suggestions for making, will be
helpful:

*Book bag*—Take a piece of blue or brown denim, or gray
linen, fifteen inches wide and thirty long.    Outline a simple
conventional design on one or both sides, with rope linen.
Sew up in the shape of a bag and bind around the top.
Three inches from the top put in a casing, through which
run a cord or ribbon, by which to carry the bag.

*Marble bag*—Take a piece of bright striped ticking or
cretonne, and make a bag four inches wide by five inches
long, turn down a narrow hem at the top, through which run
a strong cord.

A *Laundry bag* is made of gray linen and has the words
"Collars and Cuffs" or " Handkerchiefs" outlined upon one

side. For larger pieces the common grain bags with the word "Laundry" outlined in turkey red, and two rings sewed on by which to hang them up, are sensible and durable.

Dainty *bags* for *thimble parties* are made by taking a pretty silk handkerchief or square of silk, around which sew an edge of lace an inch and a half wide. Trace a circle around the handkerchief, leaving enough space all around for a frill, and put in a casing of ribbon to match the handkerchief, through which run narrow ribbon of contrasting color.

*Party bags* may be made the shape of an old-fashioned purse, with sliding rings, or like the ordinary shopping bags. For these, black corded silk or heavy satin outlined with gold thread are pretty and serviceable.

*Opera-glass bags* of fancy ribbon, plush or silk, cut to fit the glasses, and shirred across the top, are convenient and dainty to carry.

A *pretty shopping bag* is made by sewing together, lengthwise, on the wrong side, three lengths of velvet ribbon and two of satin (alternating them,) of equal width and of any desired color. When sewed, fold crosswise, sew up, leaving a heading and shirring, through which run ribbon or cord.

The small, bright striped cotton towels to be found at any dry goods store make pretty *dust bags*. For the dust-cloth take three quarters of a yard of cheese-cloth and fringe out half an inch on each side.

*Satchel bags*, in odd shapes and of pretty colored ribbon or silk, are inexpensive and are welcome additions to every lady's or gentleman's apartments.

*Shoe bags, stocking bags* and *patch bags* of cretonne or

ticking cost but a trifle. and encourage the habit of having
"a place for everything."

In addition to the above may be added knitting bags,
game bags. clothes-pin bags, button and spool bags, fan
bags. chamois skin bags for watches and jewelry, travelling
bags, handkerchief bags, and card and photo bags.

### Presidential Cabinet in 1900.

Let a young lady, who is a fluent talker, give an exhibition of "wax works," consisting of the President of the
United States and *her* cabinet in 1900.

She should first give a talk on "Woman's Rights," urg-
ing the necessity of the affairs of state and nation being con-
trolled by "wimmen." She then gives a description of the
White House. and sings the praises of her candidate for
President as she will take her place in 1900. While she is
talking. the candidate "moves in" as if automatically, and
takes her place in the middle of the platform where she
remains motionless.

As the qualifications of each Cabinet officer are stated.
she "moves in" in the same way, taking her place to the
right or left of the President. fully equipped for the work of
her department.

A small girl is on hand with a large oil-can. her duty
being to keep the "figures" well oiled and "wound up."

The speaker continues her address, (the "figures" mean-
time automatically going through the work of their several
departments.) crying down the evils of the day. stating the
utter inability of the "men folks," to bring about a better
state of affairs. and concludes by assuring her hearers of the
"good times coming." when "wimmen shall be at the helm."

## Little Old Folks' Concert.

Children's work is always pleasing. This concert is a little out of the ordinary, and is full of interest both to the children and their friends.

Have a large chorus of boys and girls. The boys wear spike tail coats, three-cornered hats, brocade vests and knee pants, and low shoes with buckles.

The girls wear wide, full skirts, tight bodices with puffed sleeves, poke bonnets, glasses, etc., and carry huge hand-bags or umbrellas.

Have one of the boys in faultless costume drilled as a leader for the choruses, using a baton and music rack.

Quartets, duets and solos will complete a program, which is much the same as for *any* old folks' concert.

The following songs are pretty for children's voices: "Old Folks at Home," "Auld Lang Syne," "Cousin Jedediah," "Revolutionary Tea," and "Grandma's Advice."

The song, "The Three Old Maids of Lee," can be used nicely in this concert. Let one girl sing the song, and after the first verse have a tableau to represent the three "fair young maids of Lee," and after the last verse another, to represent the

"Three *old* maids of Lee,
They were cross as cross could be."

Four boys will act as ushers and distribute programs. By all means sell tickets in advance.

❖ — — —

## Calico Party.

The time for giving a Calico Party is in the fall—the place a large modern attic or a barn.

Written or printed invitations are issued. On the

envelope containing the same. paste bits of calico of various colors, in different shapes—squares, stars and crescents.

Where the party is held have festoons of leaves and vines, heaps of corn stalks, piles of pumpkins and cabbage, and large baskets of autumn fruits, with here and there a "jack-o'-lantern."

The ladies participating wear bright gowns of calico or cretonne. Gowns of plain blue, red, orange or green calico are also in place.

For amusement, have an "apple paring" or a "husking bee."

Serve lunch, consisting of pumpkin pie. apples, ginger-bread and milk, and nuts.

Decorate the tables with golden rod, bitter sweet berries and bright hued leaves.

After lunch, games or conversation complete the evening's festivities.

### International Congress.

This entertainment is arranged and conducted much the same as a bazar. Booths are arranged and presided over by representatives from the different countries, in appropriate costume.

A different bill of fare is served in each booth.

In the Japanese booth, rice and tea are served, and Japanese articles are offered for sale.

In the German booth, sauer kraut, pretzels, rye bread and Dutch cheese are served, and so on in all the booths.

A representative from each country takes part in the program. and as many countries should be represented as possible. This will afford a varied program, and a unique and pleasing entertainment.

An admission fee is charged at the door, refreshments being served at the different booths, for which a separate charge is made.

— ❖

## Bonnet and Necktie Party.

For an evening of fun and real sociability, let all who have not yet done so, try the Bonnet and Necktie Party.

Invite a large number of *young* people of all ages. Instruct the ladies to bring an untrimmed hat or bonnet of any kind. - the more old-fashioned, the better—also enough suitable materials for trimming the same. For the latter, flowers, feathers, ornaments and ribbon will be necessary for a stylish "trim." Each lady must also provide thread, needles, scissors, and two thimbles. Instruct each gentleman who attends, to buy or beg sufficient material for a necktie of any kind or style.

Upon arriving, each lady leaves her bonnet and trimming on a table provided for the purpose, and each gentleman his material for a necktie, on another.

Have prepared two baskets of cards with corresponding numbers, one for ladies, the other for gentlemen. After each guest has chosen a card let the numbers be called. The lady and gentleman holding No. 1 come forward to the tables, where the lady selects material for a necktie that she thinks would be becoming to her partner, and he selects a bonnet and material for trimming, that he thinks she would consider "a love of a bonnet." They then find seats and the work and fun begins.

No. 2 is next called, and so on till all are supplied. A half hour or an hour is allowed for the work, at the end of which time it must be done. No help or suggestions are allowed, each person being required to use his own taste and skill.

At the expiration of the time allowed, each person presents, in a neat little speech, the bonnet or necktie to his partner, and all must wear them during the evening.

A committee of non-contestants determines which couple has done the most satisfactory work, said couple to lead in the grand march that follows, also to occupy the place of honor at the supper table.

—— ❖ ———— —

### Autumnal Fete.

This is a most pleasing entertainment, gotten up with little expense, and may continue through several days and evenings.

A number of booths are arranged, some serving as lunch rooms, others containing articles for sale.

A *corn booth* is made pretty with decorations of cornstalks, a pyramid of corn (on the ear) and festoons of strung popcorn. Parched sweet corn, canned and dried corn, popcorn and popcorn balls, door-mats made of cornhusks, thermometer cases, made by bronzing an ear of corn, removing enough of the grains to insert a little thermometer, and hung up by a fancy ribbon, will all be found in this booth. Bangle boards, made by inserting a row of hooks in an ear of corn (bronzed) and hung up by a small chain or ribbon, are also pretty.

Another booth, sure of being well patronized, is the *sugar house*, containing home-made candies.

One of the booths, the *fruit market*, contains small baskets of choice apples, peaches, plums and grapes, to be sold at twenty-five cents each. Small pumpkin and apple pies are also offered at this booth as well as pumpkins and squash.

Another booth which receives special attention should be decorated with woodbine, wild clematis, etc., and should have on sale bunches of goldenrod, bitter-sweet berries, milkweed pompons, bunches of cat-tails, dried grasses, etc. These are all desirable for winter house decorations, and many will be glad of obtaining them in this way.

If a program is given the platform should be nicely decorated with sheaves of wheat, large branches of forest trees, cornstalks, pumpkins, and baskets of autumn fruits.

Every number on the program pertains to autumn—autumnal fruits, flowers, sports, etc.

Dinners and suppers may be served each day of the fete.

## Old Folkes Synging Meeting.

### A LYSTE OF YE PYECES.

#### PART YE FIRST.

1. Auld Lang Syne - All ye men and wimmen.
2. Sherburne - All ye men and wimmen.
3. Olde Folkes at Home - - Quartette.
4. Ocean - - - - All ye singers.
5. Worldlye Song - "Revolutionary Tea" (solo).
6. Jerusalem, my Glorious Home - All ye singers.
7. Marseilles Hymn - - - All ye singers.

#### PART YE SECOND.

1. Strike ye Cymbal - - All ye singers.
2. Worldlye Song - "Grandma's Advice" (solo).
3. Home Again - - - - Quartette.
4. Cousin Jedediah - - - All ye singers.
5. Anvil chorus - - - All ye singers.
6. Olde Hundred - - - Everybody.

Admission—One English Shylling.

N. B.  Ye doors shall be open at early candle lighte.  Ye synging shall begin at eight of ye clocke.

N. B.  Ye olde ladies need not bring your foot-stoves.

N. B.  Ye small boys will not make a noise with their feet, as ye tune finder and time beater has his eye on them.

N. B.  Ye men and wimmen will be suffered to sit together for ye once.

N. B.  Bro. —— —— will attend to trimming ye candles.

N. B.  Ye younge men are requested to turn their eyes from the maidens, lest they be confused, and so falter.

N. B.  A silence should prevade ye assembly, unless, peradventure, some of ye worldlye songs be funny, in which event a little laughter will be indulged.

N. B.  All such as be endowed with strong lungs and a musickle training, may stand and syng in the last tune which ye same is Olde Hundred.

N. B.  Forasmuch as no potatoes, or beans, or homspun be needed for this year, all ye folkes who come to this synging meeting will pay ye money to ye tither, to be found within ye big doore.

## Novelty Party.

The Novelty Party is a childrens' party, each child dressing in costume, assuming any character thought best for them—the greater the variety the more interesting.

Interest as many children as possible, giving to each a number of tickets to sell.

The party may be given in large double parlors, or in a hall.  Let a number of boys in George Washington costume act as ushers and door keepers, while a half-dozen girls in Martha Washington costume, constitute a Reception Committee.

The party is entirely informal, games and conversation taking the place of a program.

Light refreshments, fruit, nuts and candy are on sale, and are served entirely by the children.

In one corner is suspended a large umbrella, under which a "little old woman" dispenses apples, oranges and "saucer pies."

A tea-room, where wafers and tea are served, is in charge of several Japanese girls.

Little Gretchen walks about the room and sells pretzels, from an old-fashioned basket which she carries on her arm.

At the candy stand is found all kinds of home made candies.

A prettily trimmed popcorn booth contains balls of popcorn and bags of same, at five cents each.

A lemonade table will be one of the chief attractions.

A grandmother should be seated in a large arm-chair with her knitting, and should converse with a little old man with his paper in hand

A Quaker and Quakeress will also be present.

The Army and Navy is represented by two little boys appropriately dressed, the one with his gun and drum, the other sailing his boat in a tub of water.

The following characters may also be represented: "Jack Frost," "Little Lord Fauntleroy," "Tambourine Girl," "Indian Girl," "Night and Morning," "Huckleberry Finn," "Gipsy Maid," "Little Saint Elizabeth," "Little Nell," "City Waif," "Child of Fortune," and many others as they suggest themselves.

A soap bubble table in charge of several Greenaway girls will afford amusement.

Buttonhole bouquets may be disposed of by several flower girls, dressed in white, with wreaths of flowers on the head.

A mystery-box table will afford no end of fun. Solicit donations of articles worth ten cents and put each in a pasteboard box, having one color for girls, another for boys.

These are put on sale, each one choosing the box they wish to purchase, without knowing just what it contains. The articles must be *worth* what is asked for them.

The "bag of luck" will also please the children. Take a paper bag and fill with candy. Tie it shut and suspend in an open doorway, at a convenient height. The children are blindfolded and each are given three trials to hit the bag with a stick. When one succeeds in hitting the bag, making a hole in it, each child is entitled to all the candy he can get. The "scramble" will be a lively one. A similar game is to suspend an apple in the same way, each one trying, blindfolded, to "take a bite."

Another funny game is "the flying feather." The children join hands and form a ring, when someone throws a feather in the air inside the ring. Each one blows at the feather. If they blow too hard it flies away—if too lightly it falls to the floor. The game consists in each one trying to blow the feather on someone else; the one on whom it lies having to pay a forfeit. During the game the players must not let go of hands.

These games, with others that will be thought of, with refreshments and the varied costumes, will afford an evening of pleasure to the children, and will net a nice sum for their treasury.

A small admission fee is charged at the door, refreshments being extra.

### Knitting Bee.

Let each member of a society, man or woman, active or honorary, who can knit or wishes to learn, be invited to take part in a Knitting Bee, the object being to make a rug.

Each person must bring his own needles, also bits of yarn of various colors.

Cast on twelve stitches and knit, garter stitch, a strip of any length, using several colors. When the strips are knitted, fold each one double lengthwise and baste.

They are then all given to one person, who dampens and presses them, sews them all together, cuts the edges and ravels, this making the rug soft and fluffy.

When bright colors are used, the effect is very pretty; you have a nice substantial rug, as large as you please to make it, and the whole society is thus knitted together.

It will be astonishing to see how nicely the gentlemen can knit. Ladies may meet in the afternoon, the gentlemen coming to tea, and for the evening.

— ❖

## Notes.

At a "Melon Social" a booth for the sale of melons is provided and watermelon and muskmelon are served with the supper.

———

It always nice to have *printed programs*. This can be done without drawing upon the treasury by soliciting advertisements from business men and women who are interested in your work. This will not only pay for the programs, but will leave a snug surplus.

———

Avoid all *objectionable features*. Chances of all kinds— "fish ponds," "grab bags," tickets on watches, pictures, etc., are undignified and unbusiness-like, and should have no place in any entertainment. There are enough bright, innocent and attractive features, without employing any of these methods to increase the funds.

At a "Kaffee Klatsch," coffee and doughnuts, or coffee and sandwiches are served, each guest buying the cup, saucer and plate from which they are served.

---

For Relief Corps the "Patriotic Festival," described on another page, is well worth a trial. "Work it up" thoroughly and faithfully, and you will be more than pleased with the results.

---

The *expenses incurred* in conducting charitable entertainments should never be more than moderate. With wise planning and earnest work this is possible. Better put the money in the fund direct, than use it for needless expenses.

---

A "Magic Lantern," with good views and a fluent lecturer, will afford a pleasant and instructive parlor entertainment for young people. Songs and recitations in connection with a number of the views will add much to the evening's enjoyment.

---

For King's Daughters' Circles nothing is prettier than a "Purple Tea," using purple draperies and large silver crosses, of silver paper, for decorations. A program bearing on the work of the Circle should be given. Each Circle can best arrange its own program.

---

"Two Minute Conversations" are an interesting feature of an evening's entertainment. Select topics of general interest, as follows: "Reform," "Woman Suffrage," "Temperance," "Sensible Dress," "Favorite Authors," "The Tobacco Habit," "Amusements," "Modern Inventions," "Society," "Charities," "Woman's Work," "Literature," "Social Customs," "Young People's Societies."

A "White Tea" is specially pretty for Y. W. C. T. U's., having all the tables and room decorations of pure white, the Y's also wearing white dresses. A program of appropriate "toasts" should follow the tea.

A "Blue Jay Social" was recently given as a burlesque. All the "bluejays" that were to be found were the J's of blue card-board which were basted upon each napkin and table-cloth, also upon the ladies' aprons and dresses. A huge blue J was also suspended from from the ceiling.

At a "Chestnut Social" the tables are decorated with partially opened chestnut burrs, while bunches of same are suspended from the ceiling. Chestnuts are also on sale, either by the quart or in small fancy baskets at twenty-five cents. A prize is offered to the one who with the fingers only is able to open a burr. Invitation cards are issued on which are outlined a chestnut burr.

*Moderate prices* of admission, also for the sale of articles, are necessary to success. Better charge too little than too much—better have a full house at a nominal fee than a "baker's dozen" at a high price. Because the proceeds are for the "church" or the "union" or the "circle" does not justify high prices. Give an honest return for all you get, and conduct everything in a business-like manner. Never let the price of admission bar any one from attending, remembering that those to whom the price is no object, always have the privilege of making extra contributions if they wish. When asked how much it costs to "get in," never give anyone reason to ask what it costs to "get out," each guest to determine that for himself.

A "Chocolataire" is a social at which only chocolate eatables are served, and chocolate in pretty little cups and saucers. The ladies serving the lunch may wear chocolate colored dresses with white caps and aprons.

For Mission Circles a "Red, White and Blue Lunch" is pretty. Have a program of missionary songs, readings, recitations and dialogues. The tables and room are decorated with red, white and blue, while the same colors may be used on the invitation cards.

At a "*Conversazione*," invite a number of the guests who have travelled extensively, either at home or abroad, to give short talks on places or people of interest in their travels. Descriptions of cities, rivers, lakes and mountains, and of distinguished people met. Curiosities from home and foreign lands may also be on exhibition.

As to the *quantity of provisions* required for a certain number, many are at a loss to know how much to provide. To such, the following list may be helpful. For a company of seventy-five:

Fourteen small loaves of bread,
Four pounds of butter,
Eight glasses jelly,
Eight dozen pickles,
Five pounds coffee,
Two gallons milk and cream,
Eight loaves cake,
Fourteen pounds ham,
Three gallons ice-cream,
Six dishes salad,
Seven dozen rolls,
Four large tongues,
Seven pounds of veal loaf,
Three dozen lemons for lemonade.

At a "Pumpkin Social" the rooms are decorated with piles of pumpkins and corn-stalks. Small pumpkins hollowed out are used for bowls for flowers for each table, while "Jack O' Lanterns" in dark corners greet the eye. Pumpkin pie and pumpkin sauce are served with the lunch.

*Children's entertainments* are always enjoyable and successful. Each child, instead of shirking work, feels that the greater part of the responsibility rests upon him, and that upon his special part depends much of the success of the whole. All parents, brothers and sisters, uncles, cousins and aunts are interested in what the children do and anxious to see and hear them.

Your *success* will depend not so much upon what entertainment you decide to give, but with what *enthusiasm* and *push* you enter upon the work of preparation. If you are determined to make it "go," and work faithfully and unitedly in that direction, you cannot fail. If however, "you don't believe it will be a success"—for this reason, or that, or the other, you need have no fears but that it will be a complete failure.

*Genuine sociability* is another important factor. To get people to come is one thing, to have them glad to be there, and anxious to come again, is another.

Have a cordial greeting and a word of welcome for all, especially those who may feel neglected, and strangers.

Do nothing to merit the reputation of a certain society in one of the western towns, which gave frequent socials, and "froze out" all who came. A young man defined them thus: "Half the people sat on one side of the room and half on the other. They all looked at each other and said nothing, and that's why they were called socials."

When entertainments are given by *temperance, missionary, benevolent,* or *charitable organization,* an attractive nook should be provided, where some one in charge will receive new members, distribute literature pertaining to the work, sample copies of official organ of society, etc., and will explain the different phases of the work, trying to interest others in it.

———— .

In large churches and societies, where socials are frequently given, it is is well to make *alphabetical divisions* of the membership, thus dividing the work and responsibility, and at the same time making each one feel that they have a special part in the social work.    Thus, the A's, B's, C's and D's give the January social, arranging the program and serving the lunch.    The E's, F's, G's and H's give the February social, and so on till the alphabet is exhausted. Another advantage gained by this method is that it obliterates social differences and distinctions, and causes each to feel individual responsibility for success.

————

There is no better and cheaper way of advertising a church or society entertainment, than by *selling tickets.* Many will purchase, desiring to aid in the work, who are unable to attend.    Others will buy for friends, and still others for those who are unable to buy for themselves.

This, however, must always be pleasantly and courteously done, remembering that to buy is not obligatory, and that all have the privilege to decline who wish to.    It is never necessary to remind any one not wishing to buy that ··you supposed of course *they'd* buy." or, ··the entertainment being for ·our church' or ·our society' you don't see how they can refuse." or, ··everybody is buying them    I should think *you'd* want some." Each one knows his own affairs better than anyone else.

In selling tickets always state the object for which the proceeds are to be used. People like to know what is being done with their money.

Give children a part in this work. There are those whom they can reach as no one else can. Everybody enjoys the friendship of children, and it is not easy to refuse them.

Let each one go to his friends, clearly explaining the object, and he will be sure to succeed.

www.ingramcontent.com/pod-product-compliance
Lightning Source LLC
Chambersburg PA
CBHW032355020726
47499CB00008B/2762